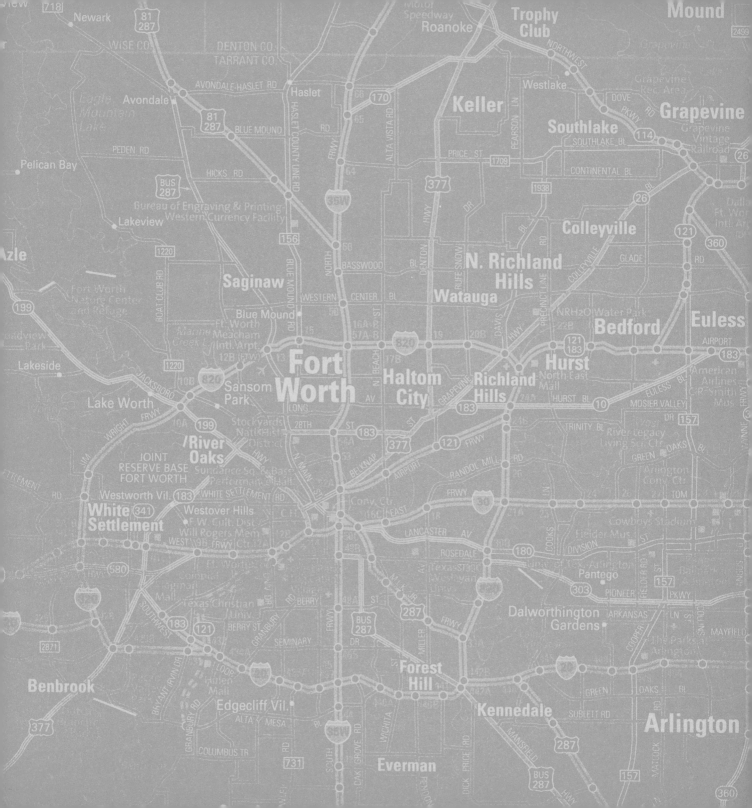

# 10 LITTLE MONSTERS

## *visit*

# TEXAS

TRISH MADSON

ILLUSTRATIONS BY
NATE HARDYMAN

# 10 Little Monsters,
feelin' a bit reckless,
take a trip down to
the great state of Texas.

**10** Little Monsters—they just can't wait
'cause monsters love the Lone Star State!

**10** Little Monsters think the Alamo's grand. They're all geared up for the trip they have planned!

One Little Monster, whose name was Shannon,
finds a booming surprise inside of the cannon.

**9** Little Monsters tour an oil rig.
One asks a question:
"How far do they dig?"

One wants to see
where all the oil goes.
What happens next . . .
nobody knows.

**8** Little Monsters ride longhorn cattle.
One Monster wishes he had a saddle.

They all yell "Yippy" and then "Yeehaw!"
And one Monster leaves to become an outlaw.

7 Little Monsters race an armadillo
from Houston . . . to Dallas . . . and then Amarillo!

One Monster simply can't keep up the pace.
He stumbles and tumbles, falls flat on his face!

**6** Little Monsters are huge football fans
and want to help out with the team's winning plans.

They're all suited up and the stadium's packed.
But after the snap, one Monster gets sacked!

**5** Little Monsters float down the Rio Grande
while visitors wave from their spot on dry land.

One Little Monster veers off to the right.
So long, Little Monster; you put up a good fight.

**4** Little Monsters see how Blue Bell is made.
They all get a sample and chill in the shade.

One Monster's greedy and yells out, "MORE, PLEASE!"
Now he is stuck with a massive brain freeze.

**3** Little Monsters love pecan pie.
They love it so much that they start to cry.
One Monster was full, but he just couldn't stop.
He ate and he ate until . . . uh-oh . . . POP!

POP!

**2** Little Monsters, just for fun,
hike Enchanted Rock to bask in the sun.
One starts to melt while enjoying the view;
now he's better known as "Monster Goo."

1 Little Monster is still on the go.
To Houston he rides for the big rodeo!
This wannabe cowboy can't seem to hold on.
With a "Good-bye, y'all!" that Monster is gone.

THE END

To *My Boyz* for their eternal support, constant inspiration, and endless nonsense. I'm grateful to be a part of your lives. —T.M.

Once again, for Henry and Hannah. —N.H.

Copyright © 2017 by Trish Madson
Illustrations copyright © 2017 by Nate Hardyman

All rights reserved.

Published by Familius™ LLC, www.familius.com

Familius books are available at special discounts for bulk purchases for sales promotions or for family or corporate use. For more information, contact Premium Sales at 559-876-2170 or email orders@familius.com.

Reproduction of this book in any manner, in whole or in part, without written permission of the publisher is prohibited.

Library of Congress Cataloging-in-Publication Data
2017941036

ISBN 9781945547089
eISBN 9781945547607

Printed in China

Book and jacket design by David Miles
Edited by Lindsay Sandberg

10 9 8 7 6 5 4 3 2 1

First Edition

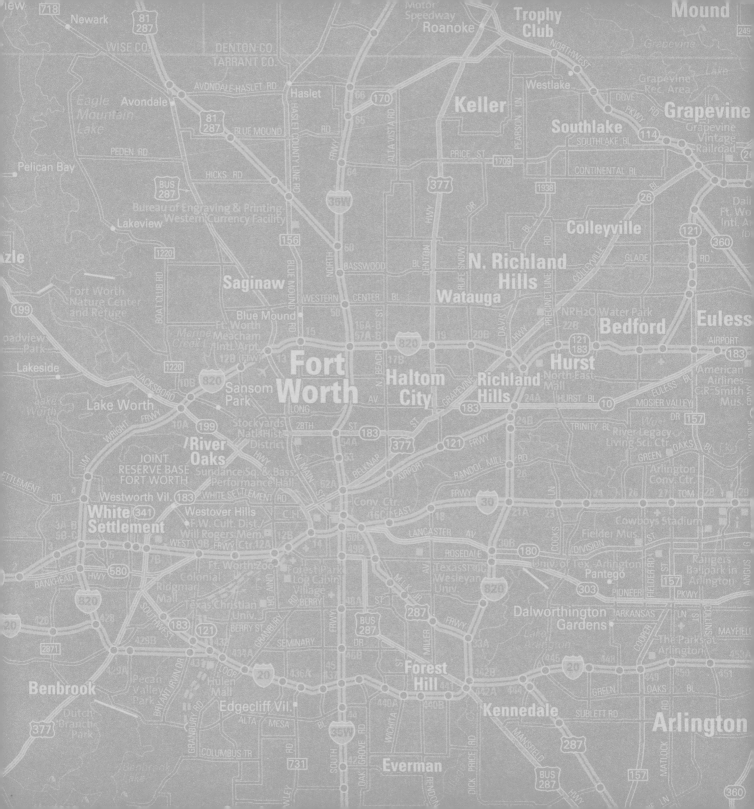